The Secret Lives of Fruits and Veggies The First Batch (BOOK 1)

By Symone Marcella

DEDICATION

For you.

CONTENTS

For information on release dates of upcoming books and exclusive giveaways, visit:

Website: www.symonemarcella.com

Chapter One:
No Laughing Matter

The world is full of mysteries, such as who built the sphinx in Egypt? Why are zebras striped? Does the Loch Ness Monster exist? How can a shark re-grow its teeth yet Grandma and Grandpa wear false ones? Since we see little birdies when we're dizzy, do little birdies see us when they're dizzy?

Why do we say 'um' or 'er' when asked a question? *Um...er!* When the light is out where does it go? What was Captain Hook called be-fore he lost his hand? Why does Dad consider everyone driving faster than him a fool and everyone driving slower than him an idiot? Do woodpeckers get headaches when they peck on trees all day long? If the planet Mars has earthquakes should they be called marsquakes? Why does a cat lift its bum when being petted? Why does a dog chase its tail as if it's never seen it before? Since plants are alive do they think and feel? Why does mum wash bath towels, aren't we clean when we use them? Why are people frightened of a mouse when it's smaller than us, yet no one seems to be afraid of Mickey Mouse who is bigger than us? Why isn't there mouse-flavoured cat food? Lightning looks like a tree branch and it also strikes trees—coincidence? Are trees vegetarian? Why do beans make us fart?

We ask questions about all of these things,

yet hardly anyone knows about the mysteries inside grocery stores and supermarkets, for therein lies a secret world…

It's a secret world that pretends to sleep when we're awake, and that *is* awake while we're sleeping. This secret world watches and waits until stores have closed for the night, and once the doors are locked and lights go out it comes alive.

Such is the case in the town of Oddfolk, which is close to the world's oddest shaped hill. It's been said that the hill is shaped like a giant lying down on one side, curled up fast asleep and sucking its thumb. This hill is known as Mount Hill Air Rios and on the other side tucked away quite neatly, is Oddfolk. The town of Oddfolk has a main road running through it called Saint Mysterion Lane. At the end of the lane is Strangeham's Supermarket, a brand-new store which will open up for the first time tomorrow morning.

However, should a curious individual find themselves sneaking out of the house at some unreasonable hour, say for instance, nine thirty at night— what's that? Nine thirty is not unreasonable? Okay, but if it's *you*, be sure not to tell anyone you're "popping out". If you find your way to Saint Mysterion Lane, you would notice that Strangeham's Supermarket looked perfectly normal on the outside. After all, the car park is empty, store lights are out and there is a large red, blue and white poster stuck on the double doors which reads:

Strangeham's Supermarket Grand Opening This Saturday.

Nothing unusual there, the only odd thing would be you in your pyjamas standing outside of the supermarket when you should be fast asleep in bed! Not to worry, let's keep that a secret, shall we?

If you were smart enough *and* a nosy parker you would try to sneak into the store…

Well you can't because the doors are locked!

Inside, the store is dark. If you were there, two things would likely catch your attention; first, a cold chill in the air coming from the vegetable open display chiller, which spans half the length of the fresh produce section and second, you would be aware of a stirring coming from somewhere within this area.

The fresh produce section is an enormous, colourful place, close to the store's entrance, home to a variety of fresh fruits and vegetables available in all colours of the rainbow. There are endless rows of produce with some loose in their boxes or sitting on shelves while others are packaged and stacked neatly on display. You would find vegetables piled on top of one another and notice a vast array of nuts and seeds; some in clear packets, others also loose in boxes. The fresh produce world is a curious place indeed, and *very* secretive.

For instance, have you ever seen a talking carrot or heard a blueberry sing the blues? Exactly! If you were there and listened *very* carefully, you might even hear…

Rustling coming from a sack of potatoes

Snoring coming from a box full of apples

A sigh from somewhere on a shelf containing

pineapples

Fits of giggles over by the cherries

And even chit-chat inside a box of tomatoes…

Ah yes, the tomatoes. This fruit (some believe it's a vegetable) can be found in an assortment of colours from red, pink and green to bright yellow. Tomatoes are smooth to the touch, fleshy internally with slippery seeds. They have an interesting combination of subtle sweetness with a slightly bitter aftertaste.

There are red Cherry tomatoes, nicknamed 'cheeries' as they are known in the produce world to be cheery and happy. 'Cheeries' are small compared to other varieties of tomato and not much larger than a grape. Green tomatoes are known to be green with envy, probably because they are packaged up and they long to be loose. Bright yellow tomatoes are generally happy, bright and don't mind being in packets. Then there are red Beef tomatoes, which are of a larger variety. They are nicknamed 'beefheads' in the produce world and considered brawny; like Tarzan or Hercules. 'Beefheads' are certainly more robust compared to say, Roma tomatoes, which are daintier, but not as petite as 'cheeries'.

Then there are the red Salad tomatoes and it just so happens that's where the chit-chat is coming from:

'If I could just get...out...of...here,' came a girl's voice. Meet Tammy Tomato.

Tammy shook her green curly fringe away from her eyes as she fidgeted about in a salad box. She sighed and fought back tears. Being in the box had left her feeling anxious and restless all day. Like all the fruits and vegetables, Tammy had been transported into the store earlier in the day in preparation for tomorrow's grand opening. It seemed to Tammy that most of the produce section were excited at the prospect of being chosen and taken home to be eaten by The People, unlike her, who longed for adventure.

She daydreamed about building a snowman inside the freezer, fishing at the fishmonger counter, water-skiing in the water aisle, admiring roses in the flower section, and then eventually leaving the supermarket to explore the big wide world! *If I could just find a way to reach the top of the box,* she thought. Her curly ponytail tossed about as she continued to shuffle around, squeezing past the other tomatoes as she made her way up to the surface.

'Oi, watch where you stick your bum, will you?' came a boy's voice from within the dark. 'I'm trying to rest.'

'I can't see where I'm putting my bum,' replied Tammy Tomato.

'Is that you, Tammy? It's me, Tom. What *are* you doing?' asked Tom Tomato. Meet Tommy Tomato, (Tom for short) Tammy's twin brother.

'Trying to escape,' replied Tammy Tomato as she wriggled to get free. 'It's too cramped. I'm afraid of getting squashed.'

Tom Tomato laughed. 'You're not a squash—you're a tomato! But maybe you'll be squished into tomato puree.'

'That's not funny, Tom,' said Tammy. 'Besides, not only do I *not* want to get squashed, I also want to be free.'

'*Wow*, sis, wouldn't that be *great*? Could you imagine if The People got to take *us* home to eat at no cost? Vine-ripened tomatoes for free, bargain! We'd be snatched up in no time.'

'I didn't mean, free of charge. I meant *freedom*!' said Tammy as she reached the top of the box.

Tom frowned in puzzlement and followed Tammy to the surface. 'But you *are* free. You're a loose tomato, not on a vine anymore. At least you're not packaged up like the cheeries and even they're not complaining,' said Tom.

'I know, but I want to see more of the supermarket. I hate being in this stupid box.'

'Well, we all hate it, but we're stuck here until someone buys us,' said Tom.

'Exactly!' replied Tammy. 'We're stuck here and I don't want to be stuck, I want to have some adventure before being bought,' she continued firmly. 'Actually, I'm not sure I want to be bought at all.'

Tom thought Tammy was joking and began to laugh. Realising she was being serious, his brown eyes bulged out and his mouth opened freely with surprise.

'But Tammy, we all want to be bought and eaten. What a waste it would be if we weren't. I mean, don't you want to provide The People with antioxidants? That's what we're good for you know. Vitamin A too,' he continued proudly.

'I know that Tom,' Tammy said, feeling cross

that he was talking as if she didn't know anything.

'And don't you want to help provide them with Iron? We're good for that too.'

'I know that, Tom. But still—'

'And how about heart health?'

'Yes, but I still want—'

'And—'

'I KNOW! I KNOW! I KNOW!' Yelled Tammy. Tom jumped with surprise.

'Shhh, you little brats,' came a whisper from

Shhh, quiet!

somewhere in the dark. 'Be quiet before you get us all caught.'

'Madam, we're not doing anything wrong,' Tammy shouted out, not realising Tom was directly in front of her.

Tom jumped up again, startled, and landed with a plop on top of another tomato, causing it to squirm. Tom heard muffles beneath him.

'Oops, sorry about that, Toby,' Tom said quickly and rolled off him.

'No one will catch us, madam,' Tammy continued. 'The store's closed.'

'We wouldn't get caught anyway,' said Tom. 'The People whiz about so much I doubt they'd notice talking produce.'

'Perhaps,' replied the cranky female. 'But you're both yapping *far* too loudly, and *I* don't like it! It's been hectic in here all day, what with The

People rushing around in preparation of the grand opening tomorrow and this is the only time when I can have some peace. As a local citizen of the fresh produce section, I order you both to be quiet!'

'*You* can't tell *us* what to do er… er… whatever you are,' said Tom.

'I'm Curtie Cauliflower. Just wait till I get my leaves on you two—then you'll be sorry.'

'Well, you won't be able to. It's too dark,' said Tammy boastfully. 'Besides, *we're* all the way over in the tomato section.' Tammy could just picture Curtie in her mind; full of leaves and rough to the touch, unlike tomatoes.

'What's your name?' asked Curtie Cauliflower.

'*I'm* Tammy.'

'And I'm her brother, Tom.'

'Well, Tammy and Tom, I think you're both *very* rude,' said Curtie.

'Are you saying tomatoes have no manners?' asked Tammy crossly.

'Yes, if the vine fits!' snapped Curtie.

'Excuse me,' came a tiny voice. 'Can someone please turn on the lights? I'm afraid of the dark.'

'Who said that?' asked Curtie.

'Me.'

'Who's *me*?'

'I'm Baby Car-Car Carrot.'

'Baby Car-Car, why are you afraid of the dark?' asked Tammy. She felt sorry for the baby carrot, as it was obvious from his quivering voice that he felt intimidated by his new environment and missed home.

'Because I can't see in the dark.'

'You can't see? Well it's tough plant pots, I'm afraid,' replied Curtie Cauliflower. 'We couldn't possibly have the lights come on.

Lights on all day *and* all night? Why… we'd spoil, and then no one would want to buy us, and then our entire purpose would mean nothing. We'd end up discarded. Discarded! Is that what you want Baby Car-Car? Do you want to be discarded?' continued Curtie.

'W-what's d-discarded?' asked Baby Car-Car Carrot, voice trembling. Tammy wondered whether the baby was afraid to hear the answer.

'It means to be gotten rid of because you're not

wanted,' replied Curtie.

'Eeek!' replied Baby Car-Car. 'But I want to be wanted. My big brother said that it's the destiny of carrots to be bought, eaten, and enjoyed so that our superness can turn The People into Super People. I want to be a super carrot, giving The People super-powers.'

'Exactly,' replied Curtie. 'And it's not just the destiny of carrots but all produce: every root, tuber, stalk, leaf, fruit, pod, flower, and bud. Besides, who ever heard of a carrot who couldn't see in the dark?' Curtie cackled.

'Yes, being chosen by The People is a common goal we all… I mean, *most* of us share,' said Tammy, yet she couldn't stop herself from thinking about the adventures she longed to experience. She snapped back to attention when she realised Curtie was trying (but not very hard) to stifle her amusement.

'The cauliflowers are laughing at Baby Car-Car Carrot,' said Tammy. 'And she had the nerve to call *us* rude.'

'Do you *mind?* We're trying to chill out,' said the cucumbers all at once.

'We were dreaming,' complained the pink grapefruits in unison.

The cauliflowers ignored their complaints and continued to laugh at Baby Car-Car.

Suddenly, there was a tremendous noise, as if several bowling balls were charging towards tenpins or worse still, a great thunderclap was rumbling.

Chapter Two: All Leaves Break Loose

'AAAAAHHH!' cried Tom. 'Tammy, w-what's going on?'

'H-how w-would I know?' said Tammy.

'You s-seem to know everything,' said Tom.

'W-well I d-don't know w-what this is.'

'Oh, d-d-dear! An earthquake, perhaps?' came the quivering voice of a potato.

'Or a t-tractor,' said a turnip.

Strawberries and grapes tottered. Many of them fell out of their bags, rolled off the shelves, tumbled down, and landed in a heap on the floor.

Celery leaves trembled. Rocket leaves shot up into the air and scattered in confusion, creating a mess.

Pineapples were shaken awake.

'My g-g-goodness, what's that great rumbling

noise? I d-d-do wish it would stop,' Puddy Pineapple complained. 'Pike, are you all right? Why won't you answer me?'

Pike Pineapple couldn't hear above the cackling of cauliflowers, the shrieking of Granny Smith apples, the moaning of melons, the screams of frightened baby spinach and baby sweetcorn, and, of course, the 'drumming' noise.

There was further excitement in the fresh produce section as the lights suddenly flicked on.

'Phew!' said a potato, which had to shout to make itself heard. 'I c-can see at l-l-least it isn't an earthquake.'

'No, it's m-much worse,' said Puddy Pineapple.

'*L-look!*'

'A stampede of carrots!' all the grapefruits shouted at once.

'They're heading towards the cauliflowers, and they look angry,' said Tom Tomato.

Dozens of carrots of all sizes—large, medium, and small—were making their way down from the crate they had been in. They marched in droves over to the cauliflowers that were still beside themselves

with laughter. A few cauliflowers—Curtie being one of them—even toppled off the shelf and landed on the ground with a thud.

'Look who's the laughing stock now,' a large carrot said to the cauliflowers.

Curtie was about to reply when she suddenly looked up in surprise. 'Great stems, who's turned on the lights? Was it *you lot*?' she asked the carrots, unaware that chaos had broken out all around her.

'No, it wasn't, Your Royal Crankiness.'

'The lights came on automatically because the carrots moved,' said Tom Tomato as he and Tammy managed to spring out of the box and bounce over to the cauliflowers and carrots. Tammy was pleased she had managed to escape the box of Salad tomatoes but not so thrilled at the prospect of facing Curtie Cauliflower. She saw that Baby Car-Car Carrot was looking around with fear at his unfamiliar surround-ings. He seemed out of place and drew close to a medium-sized carrot with long green flowing stems. Tammy began to realise that she wasn't the only one who felt uncomfortable being in the new environment and wondered whether there were many more produce who shared her anxiety.

'Speaking of lights,' said the medium-sized carrot, hopping over to stand next to the large carrot, Baby Car-Car followed. 'We came over to ask what you think is so funny about Baby Car-Car Carrot being afraid of the dark.'

'I should've thought that was obvious,' replied Curtie.

'Be careful not to upset the carrots further, Curtie,' said a cauliflower standing beside her. 'We're sorry, young lady. What's your name?'

'Carrie Carrot. This is my big brother, Cal, and Baby Car-Car is our little brother. Who are you, mister?'

'Caut Cauliflower.'

'Caut,' said Cal Carrot, 'can you explain to *cranky leaves* that it's rude to laugh at baby carrots?'

'It seems odd that a carrot cannot see in the dark,' said Curtie Cauliflower, 'especially as, when eaten, they're known to help The People see in the dark.'

'Give over, Curtie,' said Cal. 'He's just a baby.'

'Oh, I *see*,' teased Curtie Cauliflower.

'Never mind who can see in the dark and who can't,' said Tammy Tomato. 'Look, everyone! Can't you *see* the mess we've made?'

Chapter Three:
The Blame Game

'Oh dear!' said Caut Cauliflower. 'We should've been more careful. The People may not want to buy us now.'

'Eeek!' cried Baby Car-Car Carrot. 'The People won't want to buy *me*? Then what will become of me, of all of us?' Baby Car-Car Carrot wept.

Carrie Carrot nuzzled his cheek with hers. 'There, there now. It'll be fine,' she said.

'Will it? I say blame the carrots!' said Curtie Cauliflower. 'If they hadn't been trampling about, this wouldn't have happened.'

'Blame *us*?' shouted Cal. 'If *you* hadn't laughed at my little brother, we wouldn't have needed to *trample* about. And you *still* haven't apologised to him.'

'Baby Car-Car wanted the lights on,' said Curtie in a huff. '*We* cauliflowers prefer them *off.*'

'They *were* off,' said Tom. 'Yet you were still
complaining.'

'Only because you and your sister were making
such a noise,' replied Curtie. 'Actually, it's partly
your fault as well as the carrots'. So, you both ought
to share the blame.'

Curtie's accusations angered the carrots. They
shouted at cauliflowers, while cauliflowers yelled at
tomatoes. Meanwhile, the Roma tomatoes were fu-
rious with rocket leaves that had accidentally landed in their box. Some of the rocket leaves were even
threatening to turn the tomatoes into ketchup.

'And we'll personally put you in aisle four—
where *all* ketchups *belong!*' they said.

Bananas told off some potatoes that had some-

how landed on their shelf during the commotion.
The onions were upset with a few garlic bulbs that
had fallen onto them.

Tammy huffed when Curtie shouted at her to
"get squashed". This wasn't the kind of excitement
Tammy had in mind. She was beginning to think
that leaving the box was more hassle than it was
worth and even thought about bouncing right back
in! Tears welled up in her eyes and her bottom lip

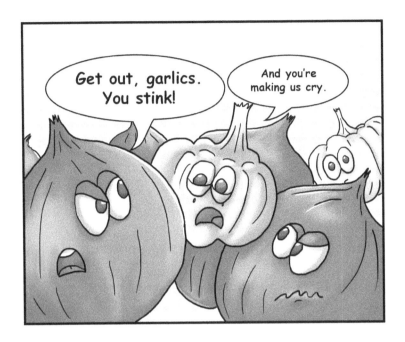

quivered as she witnessed the ongoing arguments taking place around her:

'Come to think of it,' said avocados, 'it's actually quite cold in here. We'll never ripen.'

'We'll have you know the temperature in here is just fine,' said the bananas. 'It hasn't changed a bit. Anyway, *we* don't want to ripen too quickly.'

'Actually, *we* think it's rather warm in here. We're afraid we'll sweat,' shouted bunches of spinach.

'But you're in the chiller,' said Puddy Pineapple.

'Mind your prickly pine cone business!' the spinach snapped.

'Since we're all complaining,' said a Granny Smith apple, 'I'd like to take this opportunity to say it's *still* too dark in here. Can't see to knit.'

'It isn't. It's too *bright* in here. We potatoes should be kept in the dark, or we'll be at risk of turning green.'

'Far too loud in here. One will *never* get back to sleep,' huffed a grouching Granny Smith apple.

'I CAN HARDLY HEAR A THING. YOU'LL ALL HAVE TO SPEAK UP!' yelled another Granny Smith apple.

Tammy glimpsed a brooding broccoli who hopped over to some moaning melons and joined in.

'Quite right, melons. This place has gone to the *bogs*—an utter disgrace,' said the broccoli. 'A brand-new store like this—hasn't even opened up yet—and look at it.'

'IT'S PANDEMONIUM!' yelled a bunch of green grapes.

'What? Are you calling me names?' asked the broccoli. 'Do I look like a panda's mum, whatever that is?'

'We said pan-de-mon-ium,' replied the grapes. 'You know, chaos, terrible, a disaster?'

'Obviously! This is hardly paradise, is it?' said the broccoli. 'Melons and I were just discussing everything that's wrong with the produce section. Care to join us?'

'*Oh no*!' said the melons. 'We don't want the likes of *them* joining us.'

'That was uncalled for,' said the grapes, star-

tled. 'And why, may we ask, don't you want us to join in? What's wrong with us?'

'The question is, what's right with you?' snapped the melons.

The grapes gasped, insulted. 'Suit yourselves. Are you sure you aren't *bitter* melons?' they muttered and bounced away.

Broccoli looked on in awkward silence.

Meanwhile, Tom and Tammy, Cal, Carrie, Caut,

and a reluctant Curtie had miraculously stopped arguing. Observing the chaos that had broken out around them, they decided to band together. They looked around in dismay as cabbages and parsley scrambled over to the chiller.

Cal concluded that some produce, worried about sweating, had gotten themselves into such a state that they thought hanging out in the chiller would keep them cool and prevent spoiling.

Curtie disagreed with Cal, deciding that, except for herself, the produce wasn't very clever or brave. 'They only headed for the chiller because they were too scared to stay amidst the chaos and risk being squashed or teared,' she said. Tammy heaved and shook her head at Curtie's criticism.

Whatever their reason, Caut noticed that far too many produce tried to cram into the chiller. Thus, it became chaotic there. Two types of produce seemed to each dominate a side of the chiller—spinach and turnips.

'The other produce doesn't stand a chance,' said Caut. Even cucumbers had been tossed out of their place by turnips. However, this didn't stop cucumbers from trying to force their way back into the chiller repeatedly.

'No one will give anyone the time of day,' said Carrie. 'And did you see how the melons treated the grapes?'

The group was now so huddled together that Caut had to remind them not to lean in so close, otherwise Tammy and Tom were at risk of being squashed. Tammy thought that for a moment it seemed Curtie had smirked and then etched in a little closer.

'Yes, we saw how the melons treated the grapes so shabbily,' Pike and Puddy Pineapple shouted from where they were still sitting on a shelf.

'Everyone is being unnecessarily cruel to one another,' said Tammy. 'I know we're all missing our natural surroundings and anxious about being chosen and bought by The People, but all this bickering has gone far enough,' Tammy continued, thinking that if it was this hostile within the produce section she shuddered at how things were outside of the supermarket, in the big wide world.

'Some produce doesn't think it's gone far enough,' said Tom Tomato. 'We're on the verge of war, it seems.' Tom watched the turnips shove the cucumbers out of the chiller yet again. Helpless, the cucumbers rolled uncontrollably across the floor until finally they came to a halt.

'How can we put an end to this?' asked Carrie.

However, before anyone in the group could reply, they were distracted by several more cucumbers.

'Every fruit for itself!' shouted the cucumbers as they dashed by. 'We will not be silenced. Heck no, we won't go!' they chanted making their way over to the chiller.

'Cucumbers don't give up, do they?' said Tom. 'This could carry on all night *and* day.'

'Nonsense,' said Curtie. 'It can't carry on all night and day. Just imagine what The People would do to us all if they walked into this mayhem.'

'Hey, cucumber,' said Cal as he stopped one of the cucumbers in its tracks. 'What's going on?'

'You haven't heard?' replied the cucumber.

'Heard what?' asked Cal.

'Turnips said that all produce who've resided in the chiller have spent more than their fair share in there, and the time has now come for turnips to chill out. They told us to "share and share alike",' said

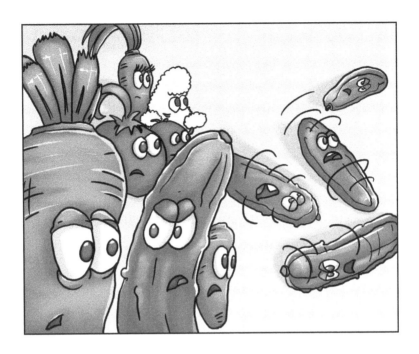

the cucumber.

'But *they* aren't sharing,' said Carrie, outraged.

'They've just tossed you all out and taken it over for themselves,' said Tammy, just as annoyed.

'I know... Crazy, isn't it?' replied the cucumber. '*Turnips* don't even need to be in the chiller, but they just laughed at us. They said there's nothing we can do, as they're one of the hardest and most powerful kinds of produce in the entire produce section. Of course, we cucumbers think that's a matter of opinion. Anyway, must dash,' the cucumber said before sprinting off to try and tackle the turnips— probably for the one hundredth time!

Further along from where the turnips had taken siege, bunches of spinach had barricaded themselves in and around the chiller, with one leaf standing at the front.

'Attention all spinach! This is Captain Spencer Spinach, your commanding officer. Hold the fort and when I say "fire", you fire those peanuts right at your opponents—which is everyone, except for us, of course.'

'What *are* you doing?' Carrie asked Captain Spencer.

'What does it look like? We're defending ourselves against potential invaders.'

'But, spinach, that's absurd,' said Tammy, in

disbelief.

'Captain Spencer, if you please. Come any closer and you'll get it, all of you. You've been warned.'

The group carefully backed away from the captain and his troop.

Meanwhile, garlic, still upset with the way onions had spoken to them earlier, bawled their bulbs out. Tears poured to the floor. The ground became so slippery that, before Caut Cauliflower could shout, "be careful", beetroot skidded across the floor. They crashed into melons, causing them to roll into Red Delicious apples, sending those flying over to the spinach army.

'Well, would you look at that?' said Curtie. 'The spinach think they're being attacked. They're preparing to retaliate.'

'You see?' Captain Spencer Spinach shouted to Tammy. 'Told you we'd need to defend ourselves.'

He turned his attention to the army of spinach. 'My fellow comrades, brave spinaches, this is it. We must strike now to defend our place in the chiller. This is a Chilling War, but don't worry, it will all be over by opening time. Remember, the only thing we have to fear...'

'Is fear itself?' asked a spinach comrade.

'WRONG!' yelled Captain Spencer Spinach. 'Angry oranges. Quick! Fire! *FIRE!*'

'WHAT? FIRE? THERE'S A FIRE?' yelled

Deidre Red Delicious Apple, who was in a daze after she'd landed right by the chiller. She either wasn't aware that spinach was about to attack or she misunderstood what Captain Spencer meant when he shouted, "Fire!"

'Heavens!' Deidre said as she sprang up, 'IF WE CATCH FIRE, WE'LL BE BURNT TO CRISPS! WE NEED WATER. HURRY EVERYONE, THERE'S A FIRE!' Red Delicious apples and sweetcorn dashed around, searching for water.

Tammy, Tom, Carrie, and Cal tried to explain that there wasn't an actual fire but, unfortunately, neither Deidre, nor the other Red Delicious apples nor the sweetcorn appeared to be listening. They were far too preoccupied trying to figure out how to put out a fire that didn't exist. It soon became epidemic as other produce began to believe there was an actual fire.

'There's water inside *us*,' said the cucumbers to Deidre Red Delicious Apple.

'We don't have time to squeeze water out of you,' said Deidre. 'But we could always throw you *into* the fire. Maybe that will work?' she said innocently.

'Rumour has it there's water on Aisle 10,' the cucumbers replied quickly before darting off, not giving Deidre the opportunity to carry out her suggestion.

'Too far. The whole supermarket would be up in flames by the time we even get there,' Deidre shouted after them.

'Deidre, cucumbers, sweetcorn... everyone,' shouted Tammy. 'We're trying to tell you that there is *no*—'

'Couldn't we leave the freezer doors open and let the ice melt?' strawberries interrupted.

'We're not strong enough to open doors,' said Deidre.

Meanwhile, Puddy and Pike Pineapple jumped down off the shelf and rolled over to Curtie and Caut Cauliflower, Tom and Tammy Tomato, Baby Car-Car, Carrie, and Cal Carrot who watched in dismay as peanuts were being set off by spinaches.

'I'm Puddy, and this is Pike. While we were sitting on the shelf pining over... well... everything,

we couldn't help but notice…'

'Notice what?' asked Curtie impatiently.

'That the conference pears seem to be devising a plan,' said Pike Pineapple.

The group studied the conference pears, intrigued by their seemingly well-organised manner. They all huddled together in their box, with the occasional nod of their heads. Every so often, a pear shouted, "But of course, yes, yes". They looked like they were all discussing something of the utmost importance.

'Perhaps we should go and talk to them,' said Tom. 'We might be able to help each other come up with a way to calm things down.'

'Good idea,' said Carrie Carrot. 'They might have a solution to stop this madness.'

Tammy cleared her throat to speak. 'Ahem, ahem! Excuse us, but may we ask what you're discussing? Do you have a plan to sort out this mess?'

'Well,' said a conference pear, 'we've just held a conference to discuss what's to be done.'

'And?' asked Tom Tomato and Cal Carrot at the same time.

'We've decided…'

'Yes?' Tammy and Carrie said together.

'We've reached the conclusion that…'

'YES?' the entire group asked impatiently.

'We've decided we don't know what to do.'

'*Oh dear*,' said Caut Cauliflower, feeling disappointed. 'That decision won't bring any of us to safety whatsoever.'

'Maybe not,' replied the conference pear, adding proudly, '*but* we've decided to hold another conference to discuss what to do about not knowing what to do.'

The group turned away from the conference pears and huddled together to hatch a plan of their own.

'Ah-ha, that's it!' said Tammy. 'Are you all thinking what I'm thinking?'

'Well, of course!' said Curtie. 'Those conference pears haven't even a *gram* of sense between them, let alone an ounce!'

'While I don't doubt you, Curtie,' said Tammy, 'what I mean is that holding a discussion with the entire fresh produce section might be a good idea.'

'Why might it be?' asked Curtie.

'We can discuss how we can all work towards a common goal,' said Tammy.

'Hmm, a common goal,' said Cal Carrot, thinking carefully.

'Yes, of course!' said Puddy. 'It's the main thing we pineapples pine for.'

'We know what the common goal is, too,' said Carrie. 'It's probably why we carrots can be quite defensive.'

'It's why I'm so cautious,' said Caut.

The group looked at Curtie expectantly.

'Well, I'm just perfect,' Curtie said confidently. The group glared at her until she succumbed. Curtie let out a sigh and hung her head, as if her pride had just taken a blow. 'I suppose it's the reason I can be a little er... er...'

'Curt?' said Caut, smiling at her with affection.

'I am what I am,' Curtie replied.

'Ah yes, the common goal,' said Tom. 'Grape-fruits mentioned they dream of it.'

'See, we all know what it is,' said Tammy.

'Including me,' chirped Baby Car-Car, bouncing with delight and feeling so clever. 'Then I can be a super carrot.'

'Sure.' Tammy smiled at Baby Car-Car before

addressing the rest of the group. 'If everyone is re-
minded, they might be more willing to work together to come to some sort of understanding.'

'Tammy, you're a genius!' said Tom.

'Hmm, I'm not convinced it will work,' said
Cal.

'Do you have a better idea, Cal?' asked Tom.

'Well, no—'

'Then I say we go with Tammy's plan,' Tom interrupted.

'Who's going to listen?' asked Carrie Carrot.

'Yes, the last I saw, everyone was on the verge
of plucking each other's stems out,' said Puddy
Pineapple.

'We just need to get their attention, that's all,'
said Tammy.

'We could always yell at them,' Tom said, bobbing excitedly at the thought of carrying out his

idea. 'Yes, let's tell them off—that will teach them.'

'I don't think so, Tom,' said Carrie. 'Telling them off will only aggravate everyone further.'

'What else then?' Tom asked, feeling disheartened that his suggestion hadn't received the kind of enthusiasm he'd hoped for.

'We can still get their attention,' Tammy said, trying to reassure Tom.

'Easier said than done,' said Pike Pineapple.

'It may not be so difficult,' Curtie said slyly.

'What do you mean?' asked Cal.

'I know just the thing,' Curtie said, a twinkle in her eye. 'Everyone follow me.'

Chapter Four:
If You Go Down in the Toy Section Today...

'Ah-ha, here we are,' Curtie Cauliflower said brightly.

The group, exhausted from having followed Curtie for what seemed like ages, looked up at a high shelf in the toy section. They saw a funny looking object which looked like a trumpet.

'What is it?' asked Baby Car-Car Carrot. 'It's *so* big and... blue, like the sky but bluer.'

'It's a megaphone,' said Curtie. 'I spotted one of The People using it this morning when we cauliflowers were being transported into the store. It seems that, when you speak into it, it amplifies

your voice so *everyone* can hear you. It also makes
the speaker sound important, too. I noticed all The
People jumped with fright when someone used it,'
Curtie continued, amused. 'When Tammy and Tom
disturbed me earlier, I joked that I'd love to use it to
get them to be quiet, didn't I, Cauty, darling?'

'Yes, dear,' replied Caut.

Tammy wasn't impressed by Curtie's comment,
however she thought the idea of using the mega-

phone was ingenious. 'If one of us stands on the highest shelf and speaks into the megaphone—'

'I'm confident the entire fresh produce section will listen,' Curtie interrupted.

'I'm still not sure it will work,' said Cal Carrot.

'Also, how are we going to carry it? It's *enormous*,' said Carrie.

'Much too dangerous for us to carry. It will crush us,' said Caut Cauliflower. 'Then we'll be flattened, and the entire fresh produce section will *still* be up in arms.'

'I don't want to get *squished*,' replied Baby Car-Car Carrot. 'Maybe if *I* use my *superpowers*, I could carry it *all* by myself,' he said proudly.

'You don't have superpowers,' said Curtie. 'You're just a baby carrot. Honestly, what an imagination!'

'Thanks for your kind offer, Baby Car-Car,'

Cal Carrot said quickly, hoping to take Baby Car-Car's mind off Curtie's remark. 'But I'll carry it. It's worth a try, I suppose. Tom, do you think you could help me?'

'Caut is right,' said Tammy and Tom together. Tom stared at the giant toy with fright. 'We can't do it by ourselves,' Tom continued.

'I have an idea, Tom,' said Cal. 'Let's go back and ask the other large carrots to help us.'

Tammy didn't like the idea of her brother putting himself at such a risk. He may be a nuisance at times, but he was still her brother and she wouldn't want any harm to come to him.

'Oh, dear boy, Tom,' said Caut Cauliflower. 'If you were a Beef tomato I'd *probably* say go for it. As it stands, you're a Salad tomato—you may get squashed. I propose someone with firmer skin. I shall go with you, Cal, and ask the cauliflowers to assist, too.'

Tammy felt relieved at Caut's suggestion.

'Nonsense, *I'll* go,' said Curtie. Before anyone could disagree, she added, 'My mind is made up. *I'm* going with Cal.'

Tammy rolled her eyes to the ceiling, thinking it was typical of Curtie to superintend the situation.

'How will you convince other carrots and cauliflowers to help you carry it?' cried Carrie. 'They're all too busy arguing with each other.'

'The cauliflowers will do as they're told. I'll make sure of it,' said Curtie.

'I can persuade the carrots to listen to me,' said Cal.

'But what about the risk of travelling back amid the chaos?' asked Caut. 'We barely made it over here in the first place.'

'How about using *that*?' Baby Car-Car squealed

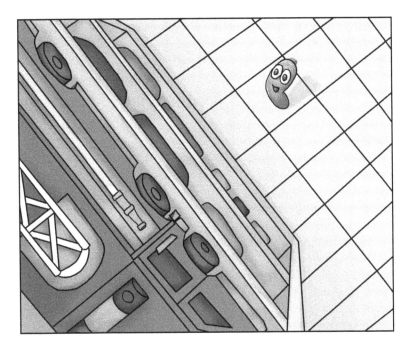

as he stared at a toy truck—as red as a fire engine—

displayed on a shelf. 'It's *gigantic*! Can I drive it? I

want the other babies to see me drive it.'

'I'm afraid you can't drive it,' said Carrie Car-

rot. 'None of us can. We're only produce, not The

People.'

'You do realise it's a battery-operated truck,'

said Curtie. 'It drives and stops *itself*. It just needs

to be switched on and steered in the direction you

want it to go. We'll figure it out, won't we, Cal!' she stated rather than asked. 'Let's go.'

Cal and Curtie hopped into the toy truck and sped off.

Chapter Five: Megaphone Mega Problems

Tammy and Tom perked up when the truck eventually returned to the toy section, with dozens of carrots and cauliflowers scrambling behind. They lifted the megaphone onto the truck, while the group hopped into the vehicle. The rest of the carrots and cauliflowers followed behind and they all made their way back towards the fresh produce section.

However, on the way, Cal noticed that cabbages and kale were involved in a bust-up. Neither party was aware they had stepped out directly into the path of the truck.

'Watch where you're going, kale,' said cabbages.

'You watch where we're going, cabbages.'

Kale and cabbages slammed into one another repeatedly, each refusing to step aside.

Tammy gulped with panic as the toy truck carrying the group, driven by Cal Carrot, headed straight for cabbages and kale, who were so engrossed with their brawl; trying to shove each other out of the way, they didn't notice the truck in time, despite Cal beeping the horn and shouting, 'Step aside!'

Tammy suspected what was going through Cal's mind. He had to make a choice: drive the truck into kale and cabbages, which would likely only anger them further as well as place the group—whom he now thought of as his friends—in danger; or direct the truck to the left and risk flattening some cherries and blueberries. Alternatively, he could steer it to the right and risk crashing into an orange stand.

As if noticing his dilemma too, Curtie yelled, 'CAL, DECIDE, QUICK!'

The truck zoomed straight for the cabbages and kale, about to send them flying higher than rocket leaves had done earlier, when, with only seconds to spare, cabbages and kale suddenly turned their attention to the truck. Their anger at almost being knocked down unnerved Cal, causing him to swing the steering wheel to the right. The truck swerved toward the orange stand but didn't crash like Cal thought it would. Instead, the sudden change of direction caused the truck to flip over. Everyone inside the truck summersaulted, and they landed with a crash.

'Oh dear, is everyone all right?' asked Caut. 'Baby Car-Car Carrot?'

'Yeah, let's do that again!' said Baby Car-Car.

'Er, no, let's not. Far too dangerous,' said Caut. 'Curtie? Carrie? Tammy?'

'Fine. We're fine,' said Curtie, agitated.

'Pike? Puddy? Cal? Tom?'

'We're okay,' replied Pike Pineapple.

'Ouch, speak for yourself,' said Tom, who spun so fast he didn't know if he was coming or going.

'Unfortunately, the same can't be said for the megaphone,' said Carrie. 'It must surely be completely damaged.'

'How do you know? We haven't checked it yet,'

Cal said, looking over to where it had landed.

'I know, but it must surely be. After all, that was quite a crash, Cal,' said Carrie.

'I knew this was a bad idea,' Cal sighed.

'Never mind that,' said Puddy. 'We have worse problems. Look over there!'

Tammy wasn't sure what Puddy was gazing at, and it seemed the rest of the group was not sure either.

Baby Car-Car blushed when he spotted more baby produce nearby. He'd hoped the other babies would see *him* driving the monster-sized truck and saving the entire produce section from catastrophe. Instead, he had been sitting in a passenger seat, only to have the truck flip over, leaving him in a heap on the floor like a helpless baby. Fortunately for Baby Car-Car, the peanuts being fired by spinach comrades meant the babies were distracted—not that he wanted them to get hurt.

Meanwhile, Tammy tut-tutted as she noticed the peanuts seemed to be enjoying the attention they were receiving from the spinach comrades. They weren't the least bit concerned about where they landed, even if it was on baby produce.

'We want to go home, back to the farm,' cried baby leeks as tears leaked down their stems. Tammy sighed with sadness at the baby leeks' distress.

'Eeek! Stop crying,' shouted Baby Car-Car, 'or you'll go all soggy and ruin.'

'Poor babies,' said Carrie Carrot, 'and the Granny Smith apples seem just as distraught.'

'*No*,' said Puddy Pineapple. 'When I said, "look over there" I didn't mean look at the babies or the grannies. I meant look at *that. Look! Fire!*'

'Honestly, Puddy, you fool! Don't encourage Captain Spencer Spinach and his comrades further,' snapped Curtie. 'And don't copy Deidre Red Delicious—she's a drama queen!'

'No, you silly battle-axe!' shouted Cal. Tammy chuckled. Tom, Puddy and Pike giggled. 'He means there's an actual *fire!*' Cal continued.

Chapter Six: The Great Fire of the Fresh Produce Section

'I can't see anything, Cal, except a little bit of smoke,' said Curtie. 'Probably Captain Spencer Spinach letting off steam. And who are you calling a silly battle-axe?'

'Look, Curtie, everyone knows there's no smoke without fire,' replied Cal Carrot.

Carrie and Caut noticed Red Delicious apples, cucumbers, and strawberries bustling around a large bucket over by the flower section, as if trying to figure out how to move it.

'Oh dear, if that bucket contains what I think it does, then the strawberries are in danger,' said

Caut. 'If the bucket gets knocked over, they'll get squashed or drown or both.' Caut gave his full attention to the concerned group of produce at the flower section and yelled out, 'YOU THERE. YOU OVER THERE. PROCEED WITH CAUTION!'

'They can't hear you, dear,' said Curtie.

'Not unless we have the megaphone,' said Tammy.

'We're way beyond trying to have a discussion with everyone, Tammy,' said Tom.

'I know that, Tom,' said Tammy. 'Cal, do you think you could still drive the truck if it's tipped the right way up?'

'Yes, if it's not broken. Why?' said Cal.

'I say we drive over to that bucket and find out what's inside,' said Tammy. 'If it's water, we can find a way to bring it back and put out the fire.'

'*Bring it back*?' said Curtie. 'A massive thing like that? Are you off your rocker, Tammy? It will never fit into the truck for a start, and we couldn't move *that*.'

'We'll cross that bridge when we get to it. Let's just get over there first,' said Tammy as she sprang out of the way to avoid being whacked by several peanuts.

'Yes, and a bridge is exactly what we'll need if the bucket gets spilled,' Caut Cauliflower muttered under his breath.

The group ducked and dived to avoid being hit by peanuts as they attempted to over-turn the truck. Cal Carrot, Caut Cauliflower, and other carrots and cauliflowers eventually managed to turn the truck the right way up. The group hopped in again, and off they went.

Eventually, they arrived at the flower section. Tammy looked up in awe at all the magnificent flowers. Although it wasn't as big as the fresh produce section, it was just as bright and colourful, filled with a sweet aroma that made Tammy feel a little light-headed and elated for a few moments. There were bouquets of red roses; some had bloomed and others hadn't yet, pink tulips, white oriental lilies, yellow roses, and mixed carnations with pink, purple and red flowers. Tammy's moment of bliss was short-lived when she heard Deidre Red Delicious Apple bickering with the strawberries about how to transport the bucket over to the fire.

'Do you know exactly what's inside the bucket?' interrupted Carrie Carrot.

'We certainly do,' said a cucumber. 'It contains water.'

'I was hoping that would be the case,' said Tammy. 'I have an idea. Why don't we get the melons, citrus family, apples, cucumbers, peppers, carrots, and anybody else who can come into contact with water without decaying immediately, to move the bucket and help put out the fire?'

'You're a genius, Tammy,' said Tom.

'Wait a minute—not so fast, *Alberta Einstein*,' said Curtie. 'How are we going to get them all to help? They're at loggerheads with each other, remember?'

'They'd better get over it or risk being burned and... *discarded*,' Tammy said cautiously.

Everybody gasped in horror, Deidre Red Delicious Apple almost fainted.

'*Oh dear, oh dear!*' said Caut Cauliflower. 'That's too much of a risk for us to take.'

Tammy and Carrie both shuddered at the thought.

For produce, to be discarded is a fate worse than what death is to The People. Being discarded not only means produce are tossed onto landfill but also left to rot and dwell on their missed opportunity to fulfil their ultimate destiny of being eaten by The People. It would also leave produce feeling dishonoured and under-valued.

Worse still, being left to rot and wither in land-fill means releasing methane gas, which The People fear may create a more toxic environment. The last thing produce want is to be a burden *and* cause ill-health. After all, they believe their true purpose is to help provide The People with good health.

There are produce, however, that believe being tossed onto landfill and left to create a toxic environment too dreadful a fate; so they choose to believe that discarded produce doesn't get ploughed into landfill at all, and are instead tossed onto a compost heap. On the compost heap, they would be left to recycle, to merge with the earth, ultimately assisting in nourishing and fertilising soil in order that fresh crops can grow.

Some produce are fortunate and get bought at a discount by staff, taken home, and eaten. In the produce world, they are known as *closecalls.* Other produce may get the opportunity to be used around the store. For instance, some bruised or slightly less than firm apples may be chosen to make apple pie in the fresh bakery section. Lettuce, tomatoes and cucumbers may be chopped up to make salads at the salad bar. Limp parsley might be used for decorative purposes at the fishmonger counter. These are known as *pickups* in the produce world.

The produce knew that if they didn't find a way to put out the fire, they wouldn't become a *closecall* or *pickup*, let alone be chosen and bought by The People. Instead they would be guaranteed a life in landfill! Tammy began to realise that even if she did venture outside of the supermarket for adventure, how far would she get before being either squashed, soaked, discarded or all three? It still might happen and she hadn't even left the store!

'We need to get everyone's attention with the megaphone,' said Tammy with a sense of urgency in her voice. 'Cal, can you take us back to the produce section, to where the megaphone fell off the truck?'

'I certainly can,' said Cal, 'but I thought it was broken. My sister said—'

'I didn't say it *was* broken. I said it must surely

be completely damaged. There's a chance it might still work,' said Carrie Carrot hopefully. She tilted her head back, stood as tall as she could, and looked over at the produce section to determine where the megaphone was. There was no sign of it and it soon became apparent why.

'Look at that black cloud,' said Baby Car-Car Carrot. 'Bet I can fly through it.'

'The fire must be spreading,' said Curtie. 'We need to hurry back and get that megaphone. Let's decide now who's going to speak into it. We can't afford to be bickering when we get there. I'd better not use it. Apparently, I sound much too cranky.'

'I don't think they'll listen to me,' said Baby Car-Car Carrot.

'I sound so serious that everyone might panic even more,' said Caut Cauliflower.

'I think Tammy should do it,' said Tom.

'We do, too,' said Puddy and Pike Pineapple.

'That's only because none of you want to do it,' said Tammy. 'Fine. Let's go.'

The group, along with Deidre Red Delicious Apple and a cucumber, hopped into the truck and sped off back to the fresh produce section, where billowing black smoke awaited them.

'Cal, mind how you drive, or we'll end up in another crash,' said Curtie.

'It's the smoke. It's so thick even *I'm* struggling to see,' said Cal, coughing. 'Seems there's hardly anybody about. Where could they have gone? There isn't even a peanut in sight.'

'Where would *you* go if you were trying to avoid being burned alive?' asked Carrie, who also began to cough due to the thick smoke.

'I'd go to the chiller—nice and cool in there,' said a cucumber.

'I can't see where the megaphone is!' Caut Cauliflower panicked.

'Over there—I see it,' said Cal and Carrie at the same time.

The megaphone was lying right by a large green crate that contained only a few parsnips. Tammy barely saw the parsnips amidst the smoke. Being related to the carrot and parsley family, parsnips sort of resembled carrots with long, tuberous roots except they had cream-coloured skin and flesh. Most of the parsnips had already left to seek shelter from the fire. The few that remained in the crate were adamant they weren't going anywhere.

'We've been here since this morning and we're not leaving now,' they affirmed, coughing and spluttering as the smoke got to them, too.

No one in the group paid much attention to parsnips, as they were so relieved to discover that the megaphone wasn't damaged at all. Now, their challenge was how they were going to lift it back on to the truck, as they were going to need the assistance of several firm produce, not just the few in the truck.

It just so happened that a group of large carrots was dashing by, and Cal Carrot called out to them for help. Soon, the truck headed for the chiller.

'Just as we guessed, nearly everyone is in the

chiller, except some of those in packages' said Tom. 'I suppose the spinach and turnips surrendered in the end. Now, we just need everyone to stop quarrelling, so we can all work at putting the fire out. Tammy, try talking to them.'

As the truck approached the chiller, Tammy opened her mouth to shout into the megaphone but found herself coughing violently and spluttering as the smoke billowed about the truck. It loomed in the air like a silent creature that couldn't be touched yet could still torment. The fire was nearby, blazing. Tammy could feel the heat and worried she would sweat but was determined to have her voice heard. She had to. She cleared her throat and tried again.

'Everyone, listen! We know how to put out the fire, but we'll need your help,' she said.

'Louder, dear,' said Curtie as she heaved, struggling to breathe.

'Oh, it's no use. They'll never listen to me,' said Tammy. 'The fire is crackling so loudly anyway,' she continued, realising she should have been more careful with what she wished for. Earlier she had wished for adventure, to explore the supermarket, but this wasn't what she'd had in mind. Now she was dealing with more than she'd care to.

'Maybe I can get their attention for you,' said Cal.

'Are you crazy, carrot?' said Caut Cauliflower. 'You're driving! Keep your eyes on the aisle.'

'You're very cautious. I'm sure you'll do just fine. Here, take the wheel...'

Unfortunately, Caut could barely see a thing. He also tried so hard to be cautious to the point where he grew nervous and began to tremble. He was shaking so much that the truck swerved to and fro, much to the group's dismay.

'My dear Cauty, you're a vegetable with many skills, but driving isn't one of them,' shrieked Curtie. 'You'd better not drive us into the fire! Cal, let Tom help you. His voice booms like thunder. Tammy dear, so does yours. *Use it!*' she ordered.

'And watch you don't fall out of the truck,' warned Caut.

'Okay, Tom,' said Cal Carrot, 'after three, one... two... three...'

'OI!' yelled Cal and Tom into the megaphone.

'SHUT IT! TAMMY TOMATO HAS SOME-THING TO SAY. IT'S A MATTER OF LIFE OR DISCARDMENT!' added Cal.

At the mention of 'discardment' everyone gasped in horror. There were screams from the Red Delicious apples, which caused baby sweetcorn to fret and squeal. Granny Smiths sobbed, melons and broccoli groaned, and conference pears huddled together as if they were about to proceed with another discussion. Kale and cabbages grunted, while pineapples sighed.

'Er… thank you, Cal,' said Tammy a little nervously. 'Hush, everyone, *please* calm down. We can prevent discardment from happening,' she continued. 'Fruits and veggies, nuts and seeds… there's a large bucket of water in the flower section. Carrots, peppers, citrus family, and melons, we need your help.'

'What do you want us to do?' asked the grape-fruits.

Tammy explained her plan, and very soon carrots, peppers, grapefruits, melons (who didn't stop moaning the entire time), and cucumbers ventured over to the bucket of water. Apples also helped. (Except for Pink Lady apples, who considered themselves far too cool and ladylike to get involved, and Granny Smiths—although one Granny Smith wanted to ride a toy motorbike and do stunts over the bucket. Fortunately, the other Granny Smiths advised against it.)

They pushed and dragged the bucket over to the fire. It wasn't easy, but eventually, they tipped the bucket of water onto the flames. It turned out one bucket of water wasn't enough to put the fire out, but it certainly helped contain it. This inspired other

produce to come out of the chiller and offer their assistance.

'Thank goodness,' said Curtie. 'It's working, but we need more water. If we could just figure out where to get more water, then our problems would be over.'

'But what about the other problems?' asked a grapefruit.

'What other problems? You mean the mess?'

asked Curtie. 'I'm sure we can all chip in and clean up before The People arrive.'

'No, I mean the freezer problems,' said the grapefruit.

'Come again?' asked Caut Cauliflower.

'The *freezers*,' added the grapes. 'One of the freezer doors was left open, the ice melted, and now there's a torrent in the freezer section.'

Chapter Seven: The Great Freezer Flood

'Oh dear!' said Caut Cauliflower. 'There's a *flood* in the freezer section? I don't know which is worse—a blazing fire or a great flood.'

'Also,' said a Roma tomato, 'all the bananas tried to escape the fire, and now they're trapped inside the *other* freezer—probably frozen stiff.'

'I'm not sure how much more of this I can take,' said Deidre Red Delicious Apple.

'Ah ha!' said Tammy. 'That's where we'll get more water—from the melted ice in the freezer section.'

'Splendid idea,' said Curtie. 'Although the strawberries did suggest that earlier. Melons, carrots, peppers, citrus, cucumbers... anyone else whose skin can take the water—get moving, right now!' she ordered.

Nobody dared to argue with Curtie. Back and forth they went, filling the bucket of water with the melted ice from the freezer section to put out the fire, and eventually it was extinguished.

'I suppose we'll be needed again to help rescue the bananas from the other freezer,' complained a melon.

'We're happy to help,' said the grapefruits at once.

'Us too,' said Captain Spencer Spinach.

'Really?' asked Tammy, surprised.

'We felt we had good reason to shoot peanuts,' said Captain Spencer, 'but it's clear now that if the supermarket is destroyed, we'll have nothing left to defend.'

'It's very risky. You're a leafy green,' said Caut. 'You do realise if you get wet—'

'Yes, Caut,' replied Captain Spencer. 'We know if we get wet we'll spoil and be discarded. Still, it's the least we spinaches can do. You see, we're partly responsible for the fire—'

Deidre gasped. Kale and cabbages growled as if they were on the verge of charging at the captain and his comrades.

'It just so happened that one of my comrades

found a box of matches lying around. I presume The People dropped it. He lit a match… poor thing… almost set himself alight.'

'Yes, along with the rest of us,' said Curtie. 'Let that be a lesson to us all.'

'Hey, shouldn't we get back to the problem with the freezers?' asked Cal.

'I suppose Tammy has an idea?' asked Curtie.

'Perhaps,' said Tammy, 'but we'll still need the bucket and the toy truck. If we could all make our way over to the freezers…'

'Humph!' said the Pink Lady apples at once. 'We'll stay here, thank you.'

The Pink Lady apples remained, while nearly everyone else made their way over to the freezer section. Even though plenty of melted ice had been used to put out the fire, the ground was still full of puddles.

'There's water everywhere. What shall we do?' asked the strawberries.

'Tammy, we're waiting to hear your great idea,' said Curtie.

'I never said it was great,' said Tammy, 'but it's the best I have right now. We'll need paper towels and lots of them.'

'We can get those,' said the strawberries, several tomatoes, and Puddy and Pike all at the same time.

'Great, get plenty of *paper* towels—not cloth towels, otherwise The People may get suspicious if they come in to find lots of soaking wet cloth towels on the floor,' said Tammy.

Tammy's theory was that they could use paper towels to soak up excess water and then pile them in a corner somewhere. The People would come into the store and probably just get rid of the soggy paper towels without a second thought. However, if they were to discover that quality cloth towels had been taken out of their packaging and used, well, it might raise suspicion.

'Cal,' said Tammy, 'can you drive them to the aisle of paper towels and then afterwards, go and find a ball of string?'

'Tammy Tomato, what's your idea?' asked Captain Spencer Spinach.

'My idea is that we need to close the freezer door that's open, so no more ice will melt. Then we need to get rid of the puddles. If we dry the floor, then everyone, including those vulnerable to water, can assist in rescuing the bananas, without the risk of getting soaked or drowned.'

'Will you be needing our help then or not?' the melons asked.

'Yes, we will,' snapped Curtie. 'And I think you know what you need to do. So, I suggest you stop rolling your eyes to the ceiling, huffing, and puffing and get on with it!'

'All right, gang,' said a melon who turned his back on Curtie and addressed other melons. 'Let's work now and complain about it later. On the count of three, one… two… three.'

Together, the melons charged over to the opened freezer door, growling along the way, as if the door was the greatest threat they'd ever come across, and flung themselves at it, forcing it to slam shut.

Everyone cheered. For the first time since being in the supermarket, melons felt a sense of satisfaction.

'Fantastic job, melons,' Caut said cheerfully. 'But please don't make a habit of doing that, will you? You could've smashed to pieces the way you flung yourselves at the door,' he added solemnly.

'So glad you said that *after* we'd done it!' re-

plied a melon.

'What's that racket?' asked a broccoli. 'I hear something, and it's very, very noisy indeed. Don't you agree with me, melons?'

'Actually, we've complained enough for one day,' replied a melon.

The broccoli hopped away, brooding.

'I know that sound,' said Baby Car-Car Carrot. 'That's my big brother in my super truck. Brumm! Brumm!'

Indeed, it was the truck with Cal and the others. They had with them stashes of paper towels and a ball of string.

'Excellent,' said Tammy Tomato, gleaming. 'Let's clear these puddles so we can get to the bananas.'

Many produce that were somewhat resistant to water grabbed paper towels. They wiped and dabbed until all the water had gone and the ground was dry.

'Oh, Captain Spencer?' shouted Tammy Tomato.

'Yes, girlie. Captain Spencer Spinach and comrades ready for service.'

'Do you think your army could rescue the trapped bananas?' asked Tammy.

'No job is too small or too great for the likes of us. Come on, sergeants. Hop to it. Hup two, three, four, hup...'

The troop marched proudly behind Captain

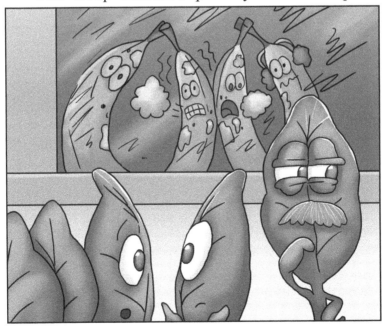

Spencer and then came to a halt. They gawped up at the freezer door towering far above them.

'Now, on my command, you know what to do,' said the captain. 'Charge.'

'Um, Captain?' asked a nervous sergeant.

'Don't just stand there, you bunch of nitwits. *CHARGE!*'

'D-do you want us to d-do what the m-melons d-did?'

'*NO*. I WANT YOU TO *RESCUE* TRAPPED BANANAS.'

'B-but we d-don't know h-how.'

It turned out that neither did the captain. He shuffled uncomfortably as an awkward silence descended.

'I was going to suggest maybe using the ball of string to help you pull the freezer door open,' said Tammy. 'Do you think that might help?'

'Why, yes, I mean… I was about to suggest that myself, of course,' Captain Spencer replied quickly.

Captain Spencer and his comrades attempted to lasso the freezer door handle. Everyone knew that wouldn't work. Eventually, the captain ordered some spinaches to "fly up" with one end of the string and tie a knot around the door handle. Rocket leaves chuckled as they watched the spinach sliding back down the freezer door.

'Something funny, rocket?' asked Captain Spencer.

'It's your comrades. They can't reach the handle, can they?' said rocket leaves.

'That's funny? I'd like to see you try,' grunted the captain.

Within seconds, the rocket leaves had shot up to the freezer door handle and wrapped one end of the string around it. Everyone cheered—all except Captain Spencer. He growled when he caught his troops bobbing up and down with excitement, celebrating the rocket leaves' success.

'Well that was just sheer luck,' the captain snapped.

'No, it wasn't. We're *rocket* leaves, Captain. We didn't mean to steal the limelight. Just trying to help.'

Captain Spencer grunted again.

'We also know there's no better produce to ac-tually rescue the bananas than your spinaches,' the rocket leaves said at once.

At this, Captain Spencer perked up and nodded. 'Yes, well, er… let's prise this door open, shall we?' he said. 'Attention, comrades. Grab the string. This is a tug-of-war: us against that blasted freezer door.'

'How bananas opened the door in the first place is anybody's guess,' said Curtie.

'Let's all help,' said Tom as he bounced over to grab the string.

'I'm a super carrot, so you can't do it without me,' chimed Baby Car-Car.

'Will the rest of you stop standing there like a bunch of coconuts and grab the string?' shouted Curtie. 'It's the duty of each of us to help!'

'Right,' said Captain Spencer Spinach, 'when I say *pull*, I want you all to tug on the string. Understand?'

Everyone shouted, 'Yes!'

'Good. PULL! *PUUUUUULLLL!*'

'Yes, everyone, pull but be careful,' said Caut Cauliflower, as he watched everyone tugging on the string.

It took several attempts, but eventually the freezer door was prised open, and everyone fell backwards, which was unfortunate for Puddy and Pike Pineapple who were at the very back of the line. Without a moment's rest, the spinach troops charged into the freezer and rescued the bananas.

'Are they all right?' asked Carrie Carrot, concerned.

'Hard to tell. They can barely speak,' replied Captain Spencer Spinach.

'W-we wanted to l-leave the freezer doors open so that the w-water would m-melt and we could p-put

out the fire,' said a frozen banana. 'W-we opened the first one fine, b-but by the time we opened the second d-door, it was s-so heavy, w-we were s-so exhausted… w-we lost our balance. S-somehow we all fell inside, the d-door slammed shut behind us, and w-we couldn't get b-back out.'

'That was dangerous yet courageous,' said Caut Cauliflower.

'Now we're f-f-*freezing*,' said another banana.

'You're not freezing,' said Curtie. 'You're no longer in the freezer. However, I imagine you'll all need to thaw out for quite a while.'

'Those poor bananas. I do hope they'll be all right,' said Deidre Red Delicious.

'Unfortunately, they hadn't fully ripened, and they're not likely to now since they've been frozen,' said Tammy gravely.

'Oh dear,' said Caut quietly. 'I think we all know what this means for the bananas.'

'Mmm-hmm! Discardment,' Curtie said matter-of-factly.

Chapter Eight:
Iced for Ages

Everyone had gasped when Curtie said "discardment" for they knew that was, indeed, the fate that awaited the soon-to-be soggy bananas.

'And by the time they've thawed out,' Curtie continued, 'I imagine they'll be watery and may

smell quite funky.'

Deidre pleaded with Curtie to stop, as the bananas began to weep.

'I can't help feeling responsible,' said Captain Spencer.

'We're all responsible, Captain. Let's hope we've learned our lesson,' said Curtie.

'Wait, I think I have an—'

'Let me guess, Tammy,' Curtie interrupted. 'You have an idea?'

Tammy was so excited for the bananas as she told them about her idea: some of them could be used to make banana muffins and cakes in the fresh bakery section or banana smoothies and milkshakes over at the drinks bar. Others could be placed on discount at the front of the store, which meant The People would see them as soon as they entered the store. They would be more than happy to take them home and make good use of them, probably to make a delicious desert like a banana split! Their skin could be thrown onto the compost heap to help nourish soil.

At this vision, the bananas began to cheer up. Tammy advised them to go back on their shelves to rest and assured them that The People would make good use of them. Everyone trusted Tammy, for her good judgement and clever ideas had proven to be beneficial to the produce section so far. They saw no reason why her latest idea would be any different.

'Well,' said Cal. 'That takes care of that.'

'I don't know about anyone else,' said Deidre Red Delicious Apple. 'But I need to go and rest, too. I'm exhausted and terrified there'll be more disasters tomorrow.'

'Us, too,' said grapefruits.

'I don't see what all the fuss is about,' said

Captain Spencer Spinach. 'Fire is out, melted ice has been cleared, bananas are saved—all is well.'

'All is well now,' said Caut. 'But it was a narrow escape. Our disagreements almost destroyed the entire produce section.'

'How can we stop something like this from happening again?' said Carrie Carrot.

'We can't,' said Caut. 'But we can take precautions and hope for the best. Any ideas, Tammy?'

'This may not be the environment we were seeded in,' said Tammy, 'but it's our new home—at least until we've been bought—so we must learn to adjust to it.'

'Why should we?' said an onion.

'Don't you see?' said Carrie. 'We need to be at our best, all of us, if we want to stand a chance of being bought and eaten.'

'She's right,' said a pineapple.

'Yes,' said Tammy. 'And if we are to be at our best, we need to look our best, which means we need to feel our best. Can we honestly say we feel our best right now?'

'No!' came the resounding response throughout the produce section.

Deidre complained again that she was exhausted, and a small banana shouted from somewhere on the shelf that it felt "dreadful and awfully cold".

'Oh, I see,' said the onion. 'If we're not at our best and our new home isn't up to scratch, The People will go to another store and we'll be… you know what.'

'Exactly!' said Carrie.

'What are we to do?' shrieked a cauliflower. 'Tammy?'

Before Tammy could respond, a conference pear came forward and cleared his throat. Tammy and Tom both suspected it was the same pear they'd spoken with earlier—perhaps the 'spokespear' for the pears.

'We've held another conference,' said the pear. 'And it seems to us that we all need to hatch a plan, create a system that benefits everybody.'

The produce nodded their heads in agreement.

'We could always entertain ourselves,' said a red pepper. 'That might keep us out of trouble.'

'We can learn about each other,' said a leek. 'That might help us to develop compassion and understanding.'

'Good thinking,' said Deidre Red Delicious Apple, 'but tonight, I think we ought to clean this place up before the store opens and The People come back, otherwise you know...'

'Yes, we know—we'll be discarded,' said Curtie.

'Please, Curtie, not the D-word!' cried Deidre.

Produce got to work quickly. Carrots apologised
to cauliflowers, who apologised to tomatoes, who
helped rocket leaves back into their boxes. Carrots,
cauliflowers, and a few pineapples returned the toy
truck and megaphone to the toy section.

Bananas politely asked the potatoes if they
could return to their sack, as many of them had re-

mained hidden on the banana shelf during the commotion. 'W-would you p-please l-leave? We need to rest and thaw out completely. We w-wouldn't want you to turn g-green either.'

The onions escorted the garlic bulbs back to their premises. 'Sorry we said you stink,' said the onions.

'You're making us cry again,' said the garlic bulbs.

'But we said we're sorry.'

'We know. These are tears of joy—you're not as nasty as we thought.'

'Well we *are* cousins, after all,' replied the onions.

Even the melons managed a few kind words to the bunch of grapes they'd insulted earlier, 'Feel free to come around and moan with us anytime,' said a melon.

'Absolutely!' said the grapes. 'We love a good gripe.'

Granny Smith apples stitched the citrus family back into their nets. Soon, the fresh produce section was completely tidy. They could see the sun rising, and its rays began to shine through the windows. Everyone had settled down back into their boxes, on shelves, and inside crates and packaging.

Well, *nearly* everyone…

Chapter Nine: A New Dawn, A New Day

The entire supermarket was filled with daylight. Curtie looked around, pleased to find the produce section was clean and, more importantly, peaceful and quiet.

'Well done, Tammy,' said the group.

'It worked!' said Cal Carrot. 'Your idea worked!'

'You also gave the bananas hope,' said Tom. 'I'm proud of you, sis.'

Tammy blushed, not that anyone—except for Tom—could tell. 'I can't take all the credit. The conference pears inspired me with their obsession for holding conferences. Just goes to show, a good discussion to work things out can do wonders.'

'I suppose we all have something valuable to add to the produce section, even if we aren't able to see it ourselves,' said Carrie.

'True,' said Curtie. 'I must admit, Tammy, you come up with some cracking good ideas. I might have been a little jealous at times.'

'What about me?' squealed Baby Car-Car Carrot. 'Don't you think I'd make a fantastic truck driver?'

'Even better,' said Curtie. 'I think you'd make a fantastic adventurer with that imagination of yours.'

The group drew in a breath at Curtie's kindness, and she found herself turning a similar shade to Tom and Tammy. Baby Car-Car barely noticed, as he was too busy beaming with pride and even seemed to glow a brighter orange!

'I owe you an apology, little carrot,' said Curtie. 'I was very mean to you, and I'm sorry. You really are brave. Sorry everyone.'

'That's all right,' said Cal. 'We've all said and done things we're sorry for.'

'I don't see what's so great about us pineapples,' said Puddy Pineapple. 'If only we were magnificent in some way.'

'I know,' said Pike Pineapple. 'All we do is pine.'

'Nonsense,' said Curtie.

'You're both very observant and knowledge-able,' said Tammy. 'As for the pining, well, I'm sure it will come in handy. As will your strength and loyalty, Cal, your nurturing, Carrie, your confidence and strong sense of direction, Curtie, your ability to assess danger, Caut, and of course, your support and love, Tom. We all make a great team, don't we?'

'Yes, but what will happen when we're bought and leave the store? The next batch of produce might create chaos like we did today,' said Caut.

'No, they won't, because we'll devise a system tomorrow night once the store closes,' said Tammy. 'And if some or all of us in our little group are sold before then, well, there'll always be someone else who'll come up with a plan. There'll always be an-other tomato like me—and produce like all of us.'

'True,' said Curtie. 'I'm not the only cranky cauliflower in the patch, you know.'

'And we're not the only pining pineapples on the shelves,' said Puddy and Pike together.

'You see,' Tammy said to the group. 'We'll be fine.'

'What about your urge for adventures, sis? Don't you still want to see the world?' asked Tom.

'Nope! There's been plenty of adventure in here tonight. I think we've done enough for today. We ought to rest, or at least pretend to, before opening hours,' said Tammy.

'Perhaps we'll speak again tomorrow,' said Carrie.

They all said their goodbyes to one another, and the group dispersed back to their new homes within the produce section.

Just in time, too, as the supermarket staff entered the store only moments later, unaware of what had taken place during closing hours. Nor did they have a clue of the greater adventures that would oc-

cur in the produce section on the following night.

But that's another story.

Fun Facts

Hey everyone, before you leave let's have some more fun. It turns out that a few of the First Batch of fresh produce you've just read about aren't quite ready to say goodbye without letting you know just how great they are for you:

Carrots

Type of Vegetable: Root

Family: Parsley or alternatively, Apiaceae (pronounced ay-pee-ay-see-ee) or Umbelliferae (pronounced um-bel-li-feri)

'Hey everyone, I'm Cal Carrot. Me, my sister, Carrie and my little brother, Baby Car Car want to share some fun facts about carrots.'

Did You Know?

• We're a root vegetable and the second most popular type of vegetable (after potatoes).

• Rabbits love to eat us. If you have a rabbit why not feed them carrot tops, a single carrot, or a couple of baby carrots. Remember, a little goes a long way!

• We come in a variety of sizes including large, medium and small; and an array of colours such as orange, purple, white, yellow and red.

• You'll never guess that back in the 1600s our leaves were used to decorate English women's hats, instead of flowers and feathers.

• There are many ways we can be consumed: Juiced, eaten raw, boiled, steamed, roasted and used in soups and stews.

• Dutch farmers crossbred red and yellow carrots to get the modern orange carrots you see today.

• We help improve your vision due to our high level of Vitamin A.

• We help to keep your body free from diseases.

• We work to maintain your heart's health.

• We carrots also work with your body to help ward off or fight unwanted bacteria and viruses.

• Eat us and we'll help clean your teeth and give you healthy gums due to our mineral contents.

• We can help heal your wounds since we contain beta-carotene.

• Consuming carrots helps to give you a healthy brain.

Cauliflowers

Type of Vegetable: Cruciferous

Family: Cabbage or Brassicacea (pronounced brass-ih-kay-see-ee)

'Hi children, Caut Cauliflower here and I would like to share with you—'

'Ahem, ahem! Caut, don't be rude. Introduce me. Never mind, I'll introduce myself. Hello children, I'm Curtie Cauliflower, the star of the story you've just read. I would like to share some fun facts about cauliflowers:

Did You Know?

• Cruciferous vegetables have four petals that grow in the shape of a Greek Cross. Our family name used to be Cruciferae, which means 'cross-bearing.'

• Cauliflowers are a descendant of wild cabbage. We used to look a little like collard greens or kale but we've evolved to look how we do now.

• We do not mind having wet leaves, so if you're growing cauliflowers, water us generously! If you cook cauliflowers for too long

it destroys a lot of our vitamins and we may let off a sulphur odour that smells like rotten eggs - don't say I didn't warn you!

• We come in a variety of colours such as white, green, purple, yellow, brown and orange.

• We help to ward off diseases in your body.

• We will provide your body with high amounts of Vitamin K which will assist your bone development.

• Eating cauliflower will boost your heart health because we decrease your risk of heart disease.

• We're rich in Vitamin C, which maintains a

range of tissues in your body and helps with keeping your eyes healthy.

• We will help your body to reduce inflammation. Inflammation is the root cause for most chronic diseases common today.

• We're great at improving digestion.

• We're full of antioxidants, which helps to protect your cells.

• We'll keep your brain healthy as we contain a B vitamin and choline, which are important for brain health.

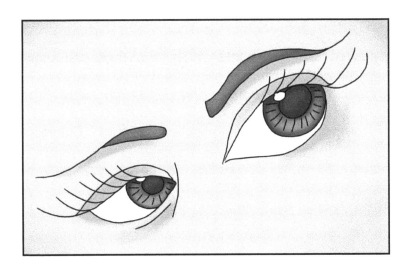

Pineapples

Botanical Name: Ananas comosus

Family: Pineapple or Bromeliaceae (pron-

ounced bro-mee-lee-ay-see-ee)

'Hey kids, we're Puddy

and Pike Pineapple.

We're so excited to

be sharing some interesting

stuff about pineapples.'

Did You Know?

• We're a tropical fruit originating in South

America. In many parts of the world we are known

by our botanical name; Ananas, which came from

the word nanas meaning 'excellent fruit'. Columbus

named us 'piña de Indes' which means 'pine of

the Indians'.

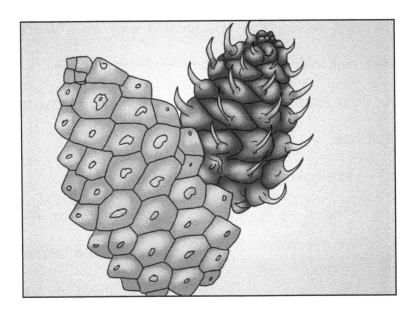

• When European explorers first came across us they referred to us as 'pineapples' because of our resemblance to pine cones.

• Hummingbirds are our most popular pollinators.

• Although you may get rid of our skin, core and ends when cutting us up at home, pineapple canneries love to use every part of us. For instance, they'll use our core, skin and end portions to make animal food, vinegar and even wine! We're delicious in fruit salads and tropical drinks too.

• It takes around two years for us to grow to full size.

• We make fantastic jack-o-lanterns!

• There are many ways you can consume us. We can be cooked, eaten raw or canned in our juices as chunks or cored slices.

• Eat us and we'll help your body to rid a common cold. We're full of nutrients including Vitamin C (aids in healthy skin), manganese (a trace mineral), copper (helps in the production of red blood cells), and folate also known as Vitamin B9 (for healthy cell function and tissue growth).

• We contain a protein-digesting enzyme called Bromelain, so we're great at tenderising meat.

• If you choose to eat us canned then make sure you choose the ones canned only in pineapple juice and not heavy syrup.

Tomatoes

Botanical Name: Solanum lycopersicum

Family: Nightshade

'Hi all, I'm Tammy and this is my brother Tom Tomato, we hope you enjoyed our adventure. My brother and I thought it would be fun to let you know a bit more about tomatoes. Enjoy!

Did You Know?

• We originally came from the Andes in South America and were first used by the Aztecs.

• Large tomatoes include Beefsteak, Oxheart and Gross Lisse.

• We're the fruit of the tomato plant, although people often think we're a vegetable. Perhaps this is because in the 1800s the US Supreme Court ruled we should be classed as a vegetable.

• We are an essential ingredient in many dishes around the world and can be used to make tomato paste, salads, juices and soups to name a few. We complement dishes that require the use of herbs such as basil, oregano, parsley or rosemary.

• We tomatoes are a treasure house of riches when it comes to health. As Tom mentioned in our story, we're high in antioxidants including lycopene. We will help to protect your body cells from oxidation and will keep your bones healthy.

• We have an excellent amount of Vitamin C, (cherry tomatoes contain an even higher amount), beta-carotene, manganese, Vitamin E, not to mention a whole host of phytonutrients.

• When you eat us, we'll help to protect your

bones, kidneys, liver, and the blood, as well as assist in keeping the body clean and free of diseases.

• We'll look after your skin and help you from getting spots. We're also a good remedy for sunburn.

• Our seeds contain lots of valuable nutrients so be sure to eat them too!

Quick tip:

If you allow us to ripen at room temperature, we should become brightly coloured and a little soft. However, if you refrigerate us before we've ripened it will reduce our flavour and we may not be able to ripen fully. Feel free to pop us in the fridge once we've ripened and just take us out one hour before use.

When choosing us, remember that we should be well-shaped and have smooth skin with no wrinkles,

bruises, soft spots or cracks. Ripe tomatoes should

have a sweetish fragrance and may give way to a

little bit of pressure when squeezed.

Lightning Source UK Ltd.
Milton Keynes UK
UKHW011543110520
363092UK00009B/1125